My Creepy-Crawly Camping ADVENTURE!

Betty G. Birney worked at Disneyland and the Disney Studios, has written many children's television shows and is the author of over twenty-five books, including the bestselling *The World According to Humphrey*, which won the Richard and Judy Children's Book Club Award, *Friendship According to Humphrey*, *Trouble According to Humphrey*, *Surprises According to Humphrey* and *More Adventures According to Humphrey*. Her work has won many awards, including an Emmy and three Humanitas Prizes. She lives in America with her husband.

Have you read all of Humphrey's adventures?
The World According to Humphrey
Friendship According to Humphrey
Trouble According to Humphrey
Adventure According to Humphrey
(special publication for World Book Day 2008)
Surprises According to Humphrey
More Adventures According to Humphrey
Holidays According to Humphrey
School According to Humphrey
Humphrey's Big-Big-Big Book of Stories (3 books in 1)
Humphrey's Great-Great-Great Book of Stories (3 books in 1)

Humphrey's Book of Fun-Fun-Fun
Humphrey's Ha-Ha-Ha Joke Book
Humphrey's World of Pets

Humphrey's Tiny Tales
My Pet Show Panic!
My Treasure Hunt Trouble!
(special publication for World Book Day 2011)
My Summer Fair Surprise!

By the same author
The Princess and the Peabodys

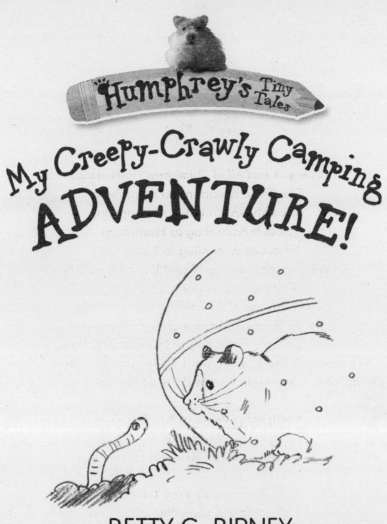

Humphrey's Tiny Tales

My Creepy-Crawly Camping ADVENTURE!

BETTY G. BIRNEY

Illustrated by Penny Dann

ff

faber and faber

First published in 2011
by Faber and Faber Limited
Bloomsbury House,
74–77 Great Russell Street,
London WC1B 3DA

Printed and bound by CPI Group (UK) Ltd, Croydon, CR0 4YY

A CIP record for this book
is available from the British Library

ISBN 978-0-571-27439-0

2 4 6 8 10 9 7 5 3 1

Welcome to
MY WORLD

Hi! I'm Humphrey. I'm lucky to be
the classroom hamster in Room 26
of Longfellow School. It's a big job
because I have to go home with a
different student each weekend and
try to help my friends. Luckily, my
cage has a lock-that-doesn't-lock,
so I can get out and have
BIG-BIG-BIG adventures!

I'd like you to meet some of my friends

Og

a frog, is the other classroom pet in Room 26. He makes a funny sound: BOING!

Raise-Your-Hand-Heidi

is always quick with an answer.

Golden-Miranda

has golden hair, like I do. She also has a dog named Clem. Eeek!

Speak-Up-Sayeh

is unsqueakably smart, but she's shy and doesn't like to speak in class.

Stop-Giggling-Gail

loves to giggle – and so do I!

Repeat-It-Please-Richie

is Aldo's nephew and a classmate
of mine.

Sit-Still-Seth

is always on the move.

Pay-Attention-Art

is a FUN-FUN-FUN friend!

I think you'll like my other friends, too, such as
Wait-For-The-Bell-Garth, Lower-Your-Voice-A.J.,
Mrs Brisbane and *Don't-Complain-Mandy.*

CONTENTS

The Great Outdoors

'What is the opposite of slow?' Mrs Brisbane asked our class one Friday afternoon.

Mrs Brisbane is the teacher in Room 26.

I am the classroom hamster.

I was thinking about the answer when Raise-Your-Hand-Heidi Hopper cried out, 'Fast!'

'That's correct, Heidi,' Mrs
Brisbane said. 'But you forgot to
raise your hand again.'

Heidi said she was sorry and Mrs
Brisbane continued.

'What is the opposite of happy?'
she asked.

A lot of hands went up.

My paw went up, too, but I guess
Mrs Brisbane didn't notice.

She called on A.J.

'Sad!' he shouted.

'Correct,' Mrs Brisbane said. 'But please Lower-Your-Voice-A.J. Now, what's the opposite of silly?'

'Eeek!' a voice cried out.

It was Gail.

She was almost always giggling.

That's why I call her Stop-Giggling-Gail.

But she wasn't giggling now.

In fact, she looked unsqueakably scared.

'What's the matter, Gail?' Mrs Brisbane asked.

Gail jumped out of her chair and pointed at her table.

'There's a spider!' she said. 'A creepy-crawly spider.'

'Ewww!' Mandy said.

Og, the classroom frog, splashed around in his water.

'BOING-BOING!' he said.

That's the way green frogs like him talk.

'Og likes spiders,' Richie said.

It was true. Og likes insects a lot.

He even likes them for dinner.
Ewww!

Mrs Brisbane walked over to Gail's
desk.

'It's just a tiny
little spider,' she
said. 'It won't hurt
you.'

I scrambled up
to the tippy-top of
my cage to get a better look.

The spider must have been tiny,
because I couldn't see it at all.

Mrs Brisbane put a piece of paper
under the spider and carried it across
the room.

Then she opened the window and gently let the spider crawl outside.

'Girls are scaredy-cats,' I heard A.J. whisper loudly.

'They're afraid of everything,' his friend Garth agreed.

I didn't think girls were scaredy-cats.

I didn't think girls were anything like cats.

I also didn't think I'd be afraid of a tiny spider.

Mrs Brisbane closed the window.

'Boys and girls, spiders won't hurt you. In fact, they can be helpful,' she explained.

I tried to picture a helpful spider.

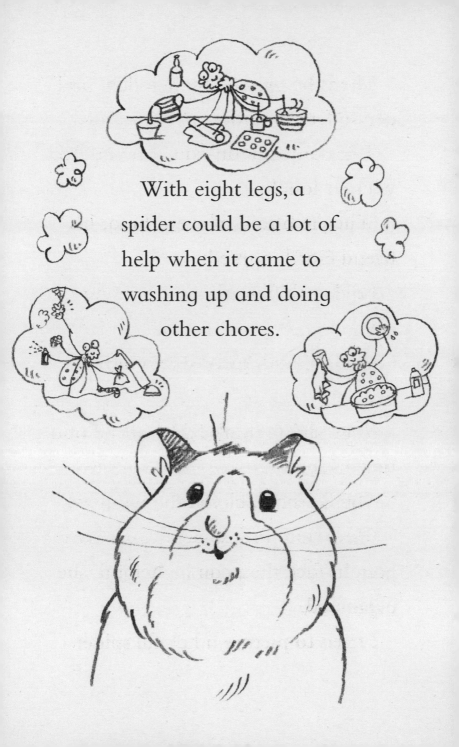

With eight legs, a spider could be a lot of help when it came to washing up and doing other chores.

Mrs Brisbane said, 'They help get rid of pests. And they're very shy.'

'But they're creepy,' Gail whispered.

Then Mrs Brisbane asked, 'Back to my question: What's the opposite of silly, Gail?'

'Serious,' Gail answered.

You know what? For once she looked VERY-VERY-VERY serious.

★

At the end of the school day, Mrs Brisbane announced that Heidi would be taking me home for the weekend.

I'm lucky, because as a classroom hamster, I get to go home with a different student each weekend.

Og the frog stays in the classroom

by himself because he doesn't need to be fed every day like I do.

'Bye, Og!' I squeaked to my friend as Heidi carefully picked up my cage. 'See you on Monday!'

'BOING-BOING!' he replied.

I think Og wished he could come, too.

So did I.

*

'Humphrey, we're going camping,' Heidi told me in the car on the way home.

'Yippee! Where are we going?' I asked.

I hoped Heidi could understand me, but I know that all she heard was 'SQUEAK-SQUEAK-SQUEAK.'

'We're camping outside in the garden,' she said. 'It's supposed to be warm tonight.'

Maybe she understood me after all!

Once we got to the house, Heidi took me outside, behind her house.

Heidi's dad was there, hammering a stake in the ground to hold up a big yellow tent.

'Welcome, Humphrey,' Mr Hopper said.

'Thanks!' I squeaked.

I wanted to lend a helping paw but it's very difficult for a small hamster to put up a large tent.

Heidi set my cage on a table.

It was nice to feel the breeze in my fur and smell all kinds of interesting smells, like pine trees and roses.

After a while, I heard a familiar voice ask, 'Is Humphrey here?'

It was Miranda, who is also in Room 26. Her name is Miranda Golden, but because she has golden hair, I call her Golden-Miranda.

'We're having a camping night!' I squeaked.

Speak-Up-Sayeh, who is a quiet girl, was with Miranda.

'I'm so glad you can be with us, Humphrey,' she said in her soft, sweet voice.

Soon Gail arrived, too. 'Is Humphrey going to sleep outside in the tent with us?' she asked.

'Yes!' Heidi said.

'Eeek!' I squeaked.

I've gone to all kinds of houses and

flats on my weekend outings, but I'd never slept outside before.

However, if my friends were sleeping in the tent, then I would, too.

Stop-Giggling-Gail laughed and soon everyone was having a GREAT-GREAT-GREAT time.

Heidi's mum and dad cooked food outside while the girls hit a ball back and forth over a net.

When it was time to eat, Miranda and Sayeh came over to my cage and gave me celery sticks and carrots.

They were pawsitively yummy!

Then, the girls toasted marshmallows over the fire.

They looked ooey and gooey.

But they didn't look like something a hamster would like!

There was so much going on, I hardly noticed that it was growing dark outside.

'Look up,' Mrs Hopper said.

Pet hamsters don't spend a lot of time outdoors.

We spend even less time outdoors at night.

So when I looked up, I was amazed to see a sky full of twinkling stars.

We studied stars in school, but I

never knew they could be so bright.

As we all stared up, Mrs Hopper pointed out that some stars were grouped together and made little pictures.

It was unsqueakably hard to see the pictures at first.

'I see the Big Dipper!' Miranda shouted, pointing at the sky.

'I see it, too,' Gail said.

I stared and stared and then I saw it, too!

'That bright star is the North Star,' Sayeh said.

'And Mars is the red-looking planet,' Heidi's mum said.

I'd heard a story about green men

from Mars invading Earth, so I was a
little worried.

But when I saw it shining, it looked
like a very friendly planet.

Then Heidi's dad said, 'Let's go for
a hike.'

'Where will we hike?' Heidi asked.

Mr Hopper smiled and handed each girl a torch.

'Right here in the garden,' he said.

Miranda put me in my hamster ball and set it on the ground.

'Let's look for night crawlers,' Mr Hopper said.

'What are they?' Heidi asked.

'Worms!' Mr Hopper replied.

'Ewww!' Gail said.

'They sound creepy and crawly,' Miranda said.

'Worms won't hurt you,' Mr Hopper explained. 'They help the soil.'

I crossed my toes and HOPED–

HOPED-HOPED he was right.

He handed the girls long sticks.
'You might have to dig around a
little to find them.'

I tried to stay close to the girls as I
rolled through the grass next to them.

Gail giggled nervously.

I was feeling a little nervous, too.

Then Heidi shouted, 'I found
some!'

All of us rushed over to the flower
bed where she was poking the earth
with her stick.

I was the last to arrive, because it's
not easy to roll a hamster ball on the
grass.

*

When Heidi shone her torch on the dirt, Sayeh said, 'Ooooh!'

'They're creepy,' Miranda said.

'And crawly,' Heidi added.

Just then, my ball rolled up to the edge of the flower bed.

I agreed. The worms did look crawly and a little creepy.

They were slimy and slithery, too.

But they weren't scary.

'Creepy-crawlies don't scare me!' I squeaked, which made Gail giggle.

As my friends were busy shining their torches around the garden, my ball hit a little rock and made a sharp turn.

I started rolling away from my friends.

I wanted to stop but the ball kept on rolling.

I ROLLED-ROLLED-ROLLED past the tent and towards the house.

Ahead of me, I saw something very long and very skinny.

It reminded me of a worm, but it

was much bigger.

It was also bright green and it curved all around, just like a snake.

'Eeek!' I shouted.

There was no doubt about it.

I was headed straight towards a great big green snake!

Boys and Noise

I ran and ran inside my hamster ball, trying to steer it away from the snake.

Suddenly, I was blinded by a bright light.

'There you are, Humphrey!' Miranda shouted.

She scooped up my hamster ball and held it in her hand.

'THANKS-THANKS-THANKS!'
I squeaked. 'You saved my life.'

'Don't be afraid,' Miranda said.
'That's just the garden hose. It can't
hurt you.'

Whew! So the fur-raising snake
was really just a harmless garden
hose.

But I had to admit that creepy-crawly creatures were a little bit scary after all!

The girls decided it was time to go in the tent.

Miranda brought me along.

It was dark outside, but it was light inside.

There were four sleeping bags in the tent and a small wooden table.

Miranda put me in my cage on the table.

There was a tall electric lantern on the table and the girls had their torches.

Heidi taught her friends a funny thing called Morse code.

She had cards with dots and dashes on them. The dots and dashes could be used to spell out words.

Then the girls would use their torches to flash each other messages on the tent ceiling by using long and short flashes.

The short flashes were dots.

The long ones were dashes.

Sayeh spelled the word 'hello'.

Heidi spelled the word 'camping'.

Miranda spelled a really l-o-n-g word.

I didn't know what it was because I didn't have a card.

Suddenly Gail shouted out, 'Humphrey' and everyone laughed.

I'd never seen my name in Morse code before.

Next, Heidi switched on a big box that played music.

Soon the girls were all dancing and acting silly.

I did a little dancing myself.

Dancing made me forget all about creepy-crawly creatures.

The music was LOUD-LOUD-LOUD.

But suddenly, I couldn't hear the music any more, because I heard a noise that was even louder.

It was a whooping, howling, laughing kind of noise.

It was coming from outside the tent.

'What's going on?' Heidi asked as she switched off the music.

'I think it's coming from Richie's yard,' Gail said.

Richie was also in Room 26 and he lived next door to Heidi.

The girls peeked out through the tent flap.

'Art and Seth are there with Richie,' Miranda said. 'And they have a tent set up in the garden, too.'

The noise was unsqueakably loud as the boys shouted and shrieked and ran around waving their arms.

Heidi turned up the music.

As the music inside the tent got louder, the boys got louder, too.

'That's it,' Heidi said, turning off the music. 'I'm going to tell them to be quiet.'

Miranda and Gail went outside with Heidi.

Sayeh took me out of my cage and gently held me in her hands.

'You come too, Humphrey,' she said.

When we got near the fence, Heidi shouted, 'Could you please be quiet? We're having a party over here.'

'And we're having a party over here,' Richie shouted back.

Then Art noticed me.

'Hi Humphrey,' he said. 'Why don't you come over here?'

'Yes,' Seth said. 'You're a boy, too. You belong here.'

It's true, I am a boy.

But Mrs Brisbane sent me home with Heidi for the weekend.

It was my job to stay with Heidi.

Art and Seth started making whooping and howling noises again.

'Aren't you girls afraid of the dark?' Richie asked.

'I know they're afraid of spiders,' Art said.

'We're not!' Heidi answered.

Then the boys started talking

about the bad things that might be
outside at night.

Art made
a scary face.
'Creepy-crawly
things,' he said.

'Howling,
growling things,'
Seth said.

'Ghost
and goblin
things,'
Richie said.
'Ooooo.'

Miranda folded her arms and walked up to the fence.

'Girls aren't afraid of anything,' she said.

'Right!' Gail, Heidi, and Sayeh agreed.

'Right!' I squeaked.

Hamsters aren't afraid of many things, except large, furry creatures with huge teeth like dogs and cats.

I'm not sure about the other scary things the boys described.

'Forget the boys,' Heidi said. 'Let's have some fun.'

*

Once we were back in the tent, Sayeh put me back in my cage again.

The girls tried to
ignore the noisy boys.
They sat around
the lantern and made
bracelets out of colourful
pieces of string.

'We should make a
friendship bracelet for
Humphrey,' Heidi said.

Gail giggled. 'It would
have to be a tiny one.'

'But he is our friend,' Sayeh said in her soft voice.

'YES–YES–YES!' I squeaked, which made Gail giggle again.

Sayeh tied a friendship bracelet to my cage, which was unsqueakably nice.

After a while, the boys stopped making noise.

It was nice and quiet.

Maybe it was a little too quiet.

'I guess the boys got tired,' Heidi said.

'Maybe they're afraid of the dark,' Gail said.

I heard some shuffling and whispering kinds of sounds.

'Something's out there,' Sayeh whispered.

'It sounds like it's near the tent,' Miranda said. 'Let's see.'

The girls quietly picked up their torches and tiptoed to the tent flap.

'There's something in the grass,'

Gail whispered.

'It's a ... great ... big ... snake!' Heidi shouted.

'Eeek!' the girls screamed.

They raced towards the house, leaving me all alone in the tent.

'Eeek!' I squeaked. 'Take me with you!'

By then they were too far away to hear me.

So I did what any small hamster would do.

I hid in my bedding and tried to be very still.

It wasn't easy, because I was

quivering and shivering.

Then I heard laughter.

I don't think snakes laugh, so I poked my head out of the bedding.

'Did you see those girls run away?' I heard a voice say.

It was Seth talking.

The other boys laughed.

I climbed to the highest point of my cage so I could see through the tent flap.

There was a snake outside.

It was VERY-VERY-VERY long.

It had a big pointed tongue sticking out of its mouth.

It was also very bright green.

And it wasn't moving at all.

I could hear the boys laughing wildly.

'I didn't think girls could run so fast,' Richie hooted.

'Or scream so loudly,' Seth said.

Art howled with laughter. 'At a plastic snake! I thought girls aren't afraid of anything!'

Aha! So the snake wasn't real.

It was a fake snake the boys had placed in the garden.

'That's not nice!' I squeaked but the boys were making too much noise to hear me.

I was upset that the boys had tried to scare the girls.

But I was HAPPY-HAPPY-HAPPY that the long green snake wasn't real!

3

Out of the Shadows

Then it was quiet again.

I knew there wasn't a real snake in the garden, but I didn't like being alone in the tent.

What if the girls forgot about me?

What if they never came back?

I heard noises in the grass.

A light was moving around the garden.

I was about to dive under my bedding again when I heard Heidi's dad chuckle.

'So that's the problem!' he said.

I climbed up to the top of my cage and looked out through the tent flap.

Mr Hopper was holding the plastic snake in his hands.

'Girls!' he shouted. 'It's safe to come outside again.'

A minute later, Heidi and her friends appeared.

'Here's your scary snake,' Mr Hopper told them. 'It's made of plastic.'

'Those boys are awful,' Miranda said.

Heidi agreed. 'That was mean.'

'It wouldn't be a good camping night without a good scare,' Heidi's dad said. 'You'll be safe now.'

The girls returned to the tent and sat around the table again.

'I'm sorry we ran off without you,' Sayeh said. 'We were so scared.'

'Let's think of a way to get back at the boys,' Heidi said.

'We could throw the snake back in Richie's garden,' Miranda suggested.

'That wouldn't fool them,' Gail said. 'It has to be something really scary.'

The girls were quiet again as they tried to think of a plan.

I tried to think of a plan, too, but I didn't really like thinking about scary things.

After a while, Heidi turned on the music again.

'Let's not let the boys ruin our fun,' she said.

Soon, the girls were dancing to the music and laughing happily.

Then, Heidi's
mum came out
to the tent.

'Time to
get into your
pyjamas and
brush your
teeth,' she said.

Heidi grabbed the big lantern as
the girls followed Mrs Hopper back
to the house.

After they left, it was quiet in the
tent.

It was lonely in the tent.

It was unsqueakably dark in the
tent!

Once in a while, I heard the boys

laughing and whispering from Richie's garden.

'Girls!' I heard Seth say.

'Let's take the . . .' Then Art said something I couldn't understand.

All the boys laughed.

Richie said, 'That will scare them!'

It sounded as if the boys were planning to scare the girls again.

But since the girls weren't around, they'd only end up scaring me.

As I sat there listening in the dark, I noticed that Gail's torch was still on the table.

I thought about the lock-that-doesn't-lock on my cage.

Humans always think it's tightly

locked, but I have a secret way I can
open it.

I knew it would be dangerous to
be outside my cage, especially in the
garden.

But if I could just flick on Gail's
torch, the tent would be light and not
so scary.

I twisted the lock and the door
opened.

I headed straight for the torch, which wasn't very far away.

Getting to the torch was easy.

Turning the torch on wasn't easy at all.

There was a button on the side which I pushed and pulled.

The light didn't come on, so I jiggled it and joggled it.

I heard a little 'Click'.

Suddenly, light shone out of the torch.

I felt much better, sitting in the big circle of light.

But as I turned to go back to my cage, I looked at the side of the tent.

To my alarm, I saw a very large, very shaggy, VERY-VERY-VERY scary thing.

'Eeek!'
I squeaked.

I raced towards my cage.

The scary thing raced across the side of the tent.

I turned and ran in the opposite direction.

The scary thing turned and ran in the opposite direction.

I stopped and sat still.

The scary thing stopped and sat still.

THUMPITY-THUMPITY-
THUMP!

My heart was pounding until I
realised that the scary thing was my
very own shadow!

I could hardly believe my eyes.

Who would think that a small
hamster like me could look so large
and scary?

I heard the boys scuffling outside
the tent.

'Sssh!' Art said.

'Sssh–sssh!' Richie said.

I knew they were planning
something creepy and crawly.

But maybe I could scare them first!

I stood in front of the torch and got

up on my tippy-toes.

Then I lifted my paws in the air
and opened my mouth wide.

I was happy to see that my shadow
didn't look like a hamster at all.

It looked like a huge and horrible
monster.

I looked like a huge and horrible
monster.

It was fun to look big for a change.

I opened my mouth even wider
and roared.

Of course, all that came out was
'SQUEAK-SQUEAK-SQUEAK'.

It was quiet outside.

I figured the boys hadn't seen my
shadow yet.

I needed to get their attention, so I
looked around.

Near me was the switch on the box
that made music.

I turned the switch and music
blared.

I pushed a little knob and the
music played louder.

I reached way up and pawed the

air like a scary monster.

And I crossed my toes and hoped
that my plan would work.

The Trouble with Monsters

'It's ... a ... monster!' Richie
shouted.

'Run for your life!' Art screamed.

'Help me!!' Seth shrieked.

They howled and yelled.
They shouted and screeched.

No matter how loud I screamed, I could never sound as loud as those boys did.

As I pawed the air and tried to look big, I heard footsteps running across Richie's garden.

'Help! Help!' The shrieks moved toward Richie's house.

The garden was quiet again.

I relaxed and stopped acting like a monster.

So, boys were afraid of some things, too!

I hoped the boys weren't too scared, but I was glad that my plan had worked.

Then I heard footsteps coming

towards my
tent.

'Eeek!' I
squeaked.

I knew it
was probably
just Mr
Hopper, but I
didn't want to be caught outside of
my cage.

Then, my friends would find out
about my secret lock-that-doesn't-
lock!

And if they did, they might decide
to fix it.

Then I'd be stuck in my cage for
ever and ever!

So I made a dash for my cage and
pulled the door closed.

'What's going on out here?' Mr
Hopper asked.

He poked his head in the tent flap
and looked around.

The torch was still on and so was the music.

My shadow was on the wall, but now it was my shadow inside the cage.

Mr Hopper laughed when he saw it.

'I think I see what happened,' he said.

He left and came back again with Heidi, Gail, Sayeh and Miranda.

'Are you sure it's safe out here?' Heidi asked. 'I could hear those boys screaming from inside the house.'

Gail nodded. 'I saw them running across the garden.'

'I'll show you what scared them,'

Mr Hopper said. 'Humphrey cast a shadow on the wall of the tent.'

He took them around the outside of the tent.

'It looks huge!' Miranda said.

'It looks like a lion in a cage,' Sayeh whispered.

'But it wouldn't scare me,' Heidi said.

'Me neither,' Gail agreed. 'Silly boys.'

The girls came back into the tent.

'I'm not afraid to be out here,' Heidi said.

'Girls aren't afraid of anything,' Miranda added.

'Girls aren't afraid of anything!' the girls all repeated.

'It's funny, but I don't remember leaving the torch on,' Heidi said. 'Or the music.'

Sayeh, Gail and Miranda didn't remember either.

I didn't squeak up and tell them I had turned them on.

The girls stood between the lantern and the side of the tent and made special shadows, like pictures on the wall.

Gail made a crocodile using her hand.

I was just a little bit afraid when
she snapped the crocodile's jaws.

Miranda made a bunny rabbit
with her hand.

It had tall, floppy ears.

Heidi made a dog using her hands.
She wiggled his ears and made his
mouth open and shut.

'Woof-woof,' she barked, which made Gail giggle.

'It's your turn now, Humphrey,' Miranda said.

I got up on my tippy-toes and raised my paws in the air, like a monster.

The girls saw my shadow and laughed and laughed.

I guess girls aren't afraid of anything after all.

When it was time for the girls to go to sleep, Heidi's parents came out to the tent.

Mrs Hopper tucked the girls in their sleeping bags.

I settled down in my bedding.

'Now, get some sleep, girls,' Mrs Hopper said as she left the tent. 'You too, Humphrey.'

★

Once we were alone, the tent was QUIET-QUIET-QUIET.

Outside the tent, things weren't so quiet.

First we heard something say, 'Whoo-whoooo.'

Gail sat up. 'What's that?' she asked.

'An owl,' Miranda answered. 'At least I hope it's just an owl.'

Then we heard a fluttering sound, like wings.

'What's that?' Heidi asked.

Miranda sat up and looked around. 'It's the tent flap,' she said. 'At least I hope it's the tent flap.'

It was quiet again – almost too quiet.

I was feeling a bit nervous, so I hopped on to my wheel.

Spinning always relaxes me.

I forgot that my wheel makes a loud whirring sound.

I don't notice it in the classroom, where there are other noises.

But in the tent, it sounded
unsqueakably loud.

'What's THAT?' Gail asked in a
frightened voice.

'I don't know.' Miranda sounded
even more frightened than Gail.

'It's just me,' I squeaked.

'Listen to Humphrey,' Sayeh said.
'He must have seen something.'

Heidi crawled out of her sleeping
bag and stood up.

'That's it,' she said. 'I'm sleeping
inside.'

'Me too,' Gail said.

'Me too,' Miranda said.

'And me,' Sayeh softly added.

'ME-ME-ME too,' I squeaked.

The girls quickly rolled up their sleeping bags and took their torches, the lantern and my cage back into the house.

As Sayeh carried my cage across the yard, I could see that the tent in Richie's garden was dark.

I was pretty sure the boys were

sleeping inside.

And even though I didn't see any real creepy-crawly creatures in the garden, I was happy to sleep inside, too.

★

When Heidi took me back to school on Monday morning, Mrs Brisbane asked her how the weekend had been.

'Great,' Heidi answered. 'I had a camping night in the backyard with my friends.'

'So did I,' Richie told her.

'Oh,' Mrs Brisbane replied. 'Were you scared to sleep outside?'

'No,' Heidi said. 'Girls aren't afraid of anything.'

'Neither are boys,' Richie added.
They weren't exactly squeaking
the truth, but I'm pretty sure they
believed what they said.

During class, Mrs Brisbane asked,
'What's the opposite of frightened?'
Richie raised his hand and
answered, 'Fearless.'

Later that night, I showed Og the
friendship bracelet on my cage.

Then I told him all about our
creepy-crawly camping adventure.

He splashed in his tank and
said, 'BOING-BOING-BOING-
BOING!'

'The girls were scared and the boys were scared,' I told my froggy friend.

'I wasn't afraid,' I said. 'At least not much.'

But I think that it's all right for girls and boys and even hamsters to be a little bit afraid of creepy-crawly creatures.

Even when the scariest thing in the garden turned out to be me!

Dear friends,

Humans love their pets, and pets like me love their humans. I'm unsqueakably excited to share everything I've learned in Classroom 26 and beyond about the world of pets with you.

And hamsters aren't the only pets! Do you know how to look after a chinchilla? What is a puppy's favourite food? As well as learning top pet-care tips, you can tell me all about your pets in the special My Precious Pet section. I can't wait to meet them!

Your furry friend,

Humphrey

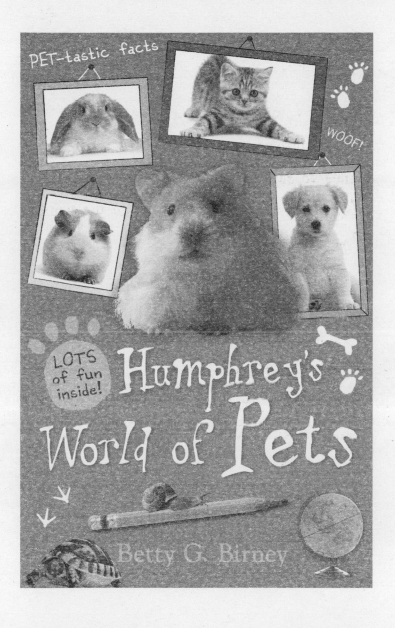

PET-tastic facts

WOOF!

LOTS of fun inside!

Humphrey's
World of Pets

Betty G. Birney

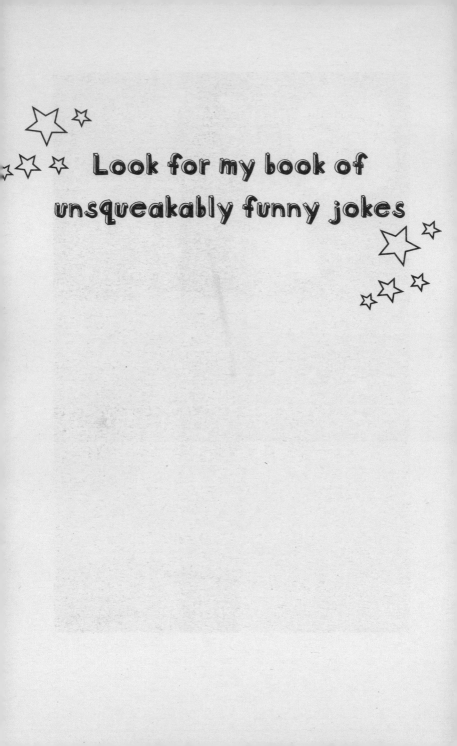

Look for my book of
unsqueakably funny jokes

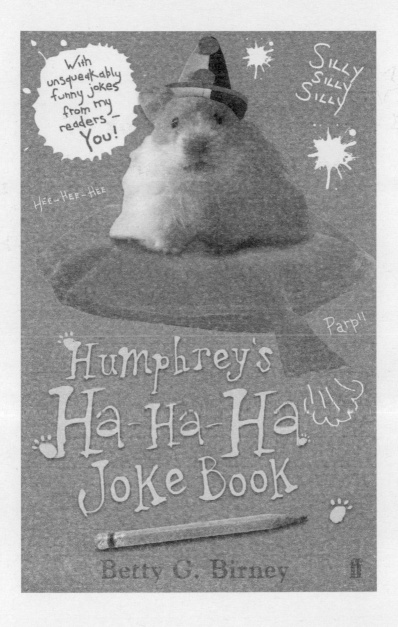

Or why not try the puzzles and games in my fun-fun-fun activity book!

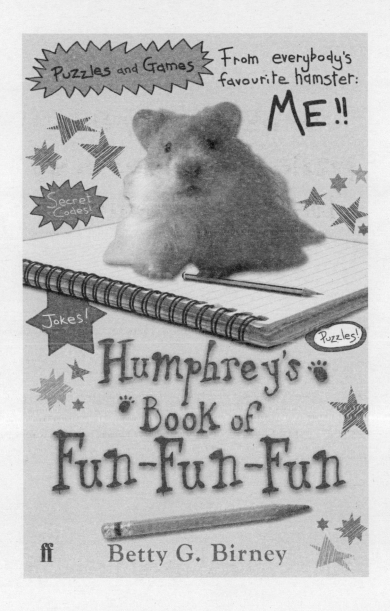

Puzzles and Games

From everybody's favourite hamster: ME !!

Secret Codes!

Jokes!

Puzzles!

Humphrey's Book of Fun-Fun-Fun

ff   Betty G. Birney

Humphrey and his friends have been hard at work making a brand new FUN-FUN-FUN website just for you!

Play Humphrey's exciting new game, share your pet pictures, find fun crafts and activities, read Humphrey's very own diary and discover all the latest news from your favourite furry friend at:

www.funwithhumphrey.com